One More Sheep

Written by Mij Kelly
Illustrated by Russell Ayto

h
*Hodder
Children's
Books*

A division of Hodder Headline Limited

On a wild windy night
in a thunderstorm,
Sam fetched home his sheep
and tucked them up warm,
with woolly socks on their toes
and woolly hats on their heads,
all safe and snug in a big cosy bed.

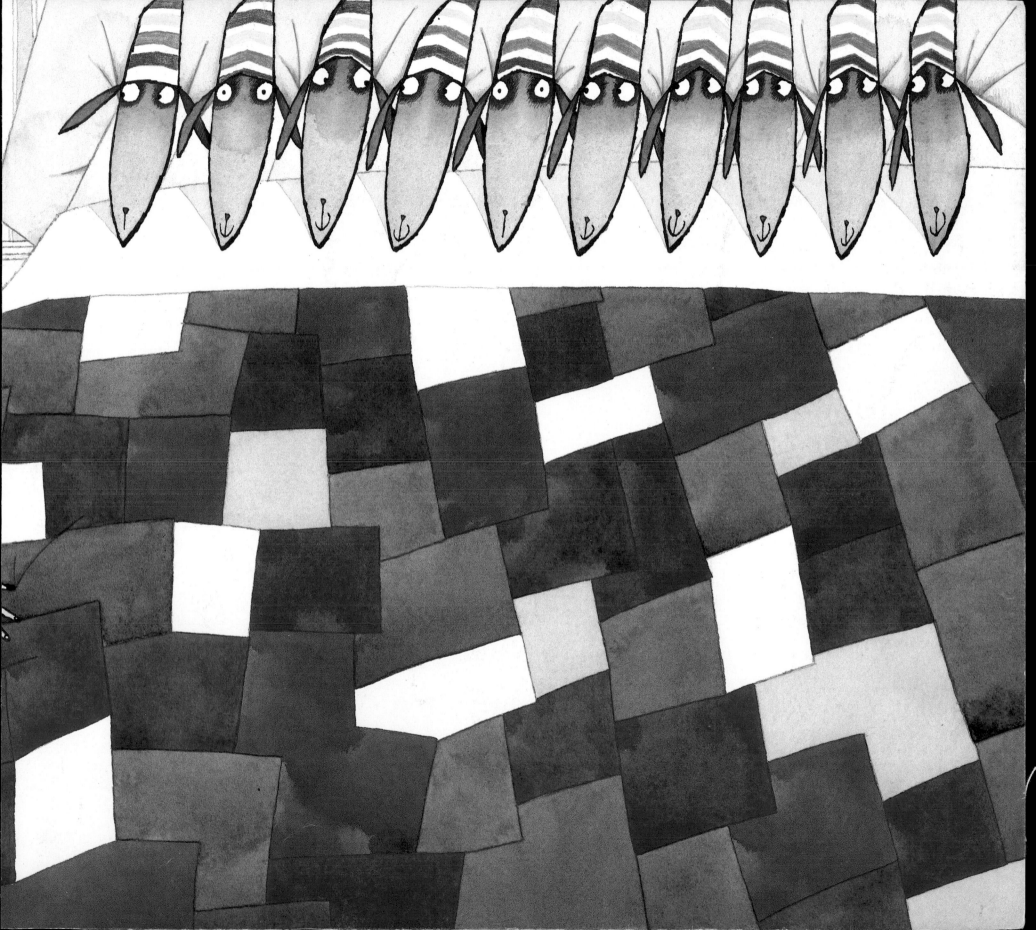

Now Sam owned ten sheep
and he had to be sure
that he'd fetched them all in
from the wet windy moor,
where the hungry wolf growls
and the hungry wolf prowls
and on wild windy nights
the hungry wolf howls.

Sam had to know
that they were all safe in bed.
And one way to know
was to count the mutton-heads.

He counted out loud:

"One...

two...

three...

four..."

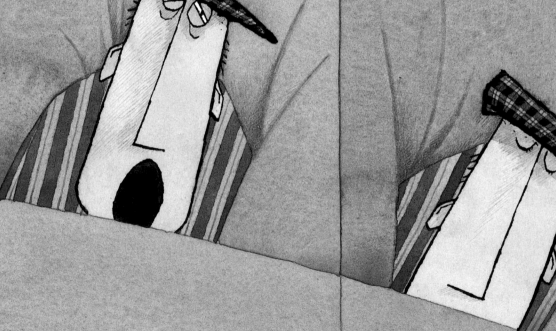
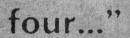

That's as far as
he got before he
started to snore.

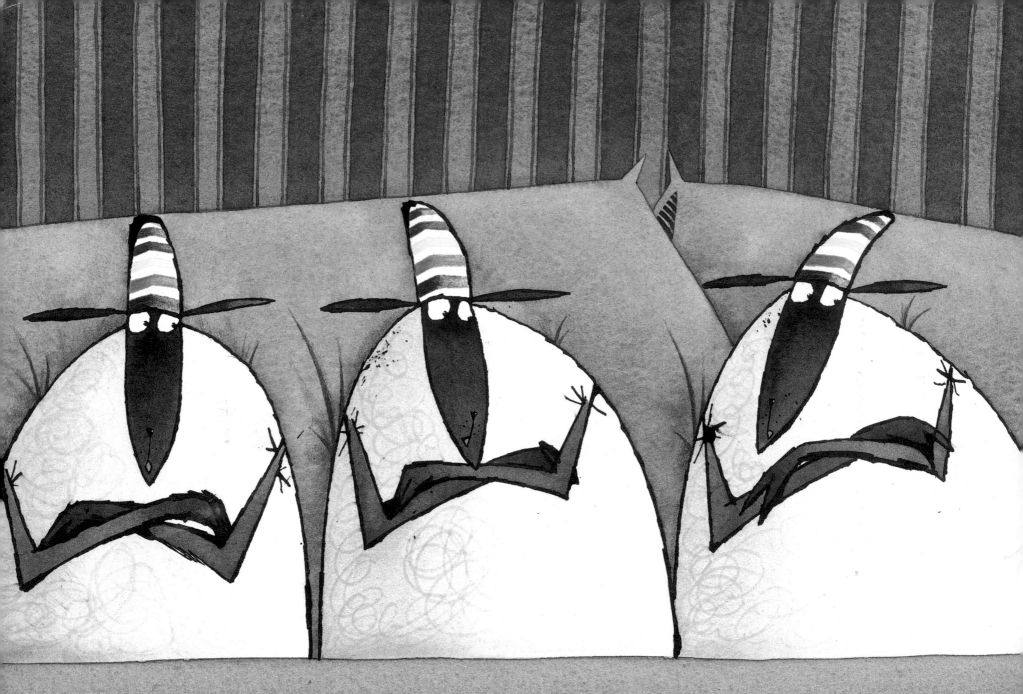

"He always does that!"

"What's so hard about counting sheep?"

"Is there something about us that sends him to sleep?"

Out on the moor
the wind whistled and wuthered,
while the sheep safe indoors
snuggled under the covers,
drifting through dreams
until a loud...

rat-a-tat
woke them all up.

"Who's there?"
"What was that?"

Sam jumped out of bed
and threw open the door.
"Well bless my pink pyjamas!
It's one sheep more,
snivelling and shivering,
bedraggled and forlorn.
What a fool I am!" cried Sam,
"to leave you in the storm.
Come on in my precious lamb."

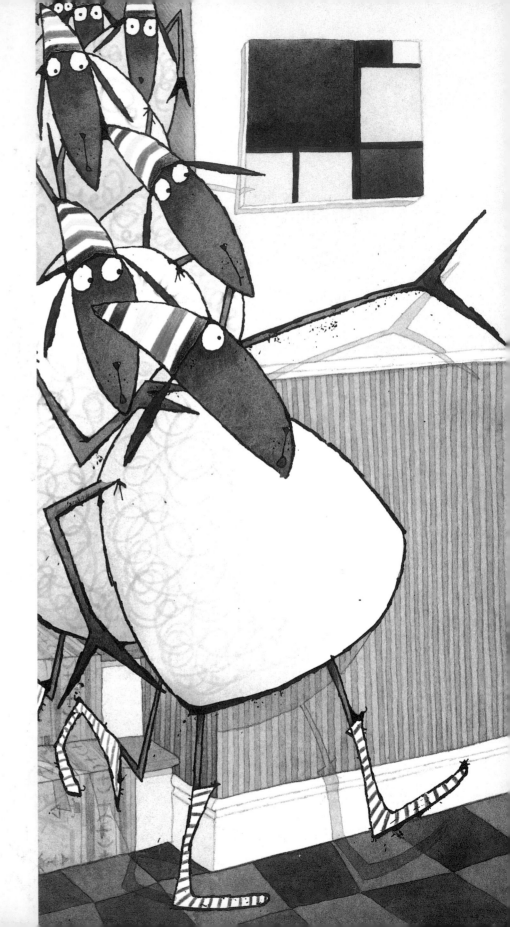

"Now don't muck about," said
Sam. "Remember who's boss.
Let the little bleater in at once,
before I get cross."

Well, Sam could count his finger
He could count his toes.
But he couldn't count the
sheep in front of his nose.
He scratched his head
and wondered what to say.
He couldn't tell them nicely...
so he told them anyway.

Sam said:
"It's a well-known fact
that counting sheep
tires people out
and sends them to sleep.

You're not at all interesting.
You're not at all odd.
You're a first-class ticket
to the Land of Nod."

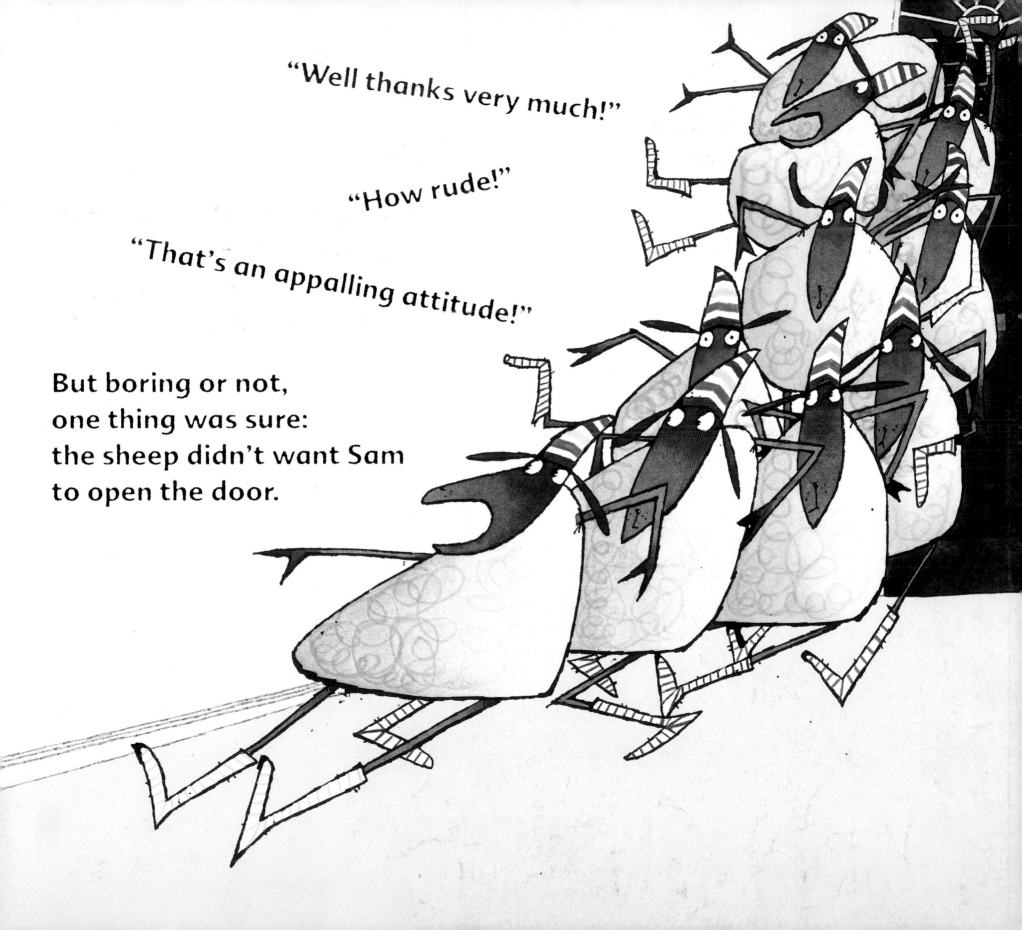

"Well thanks very much!"

"How rude!"

"That's an appalling attitude!"

But boring or not,
one thing was sure:
the sheep didn't want Sam
to open the door.

"Who's this then?"

Sam quickly shut the door again.

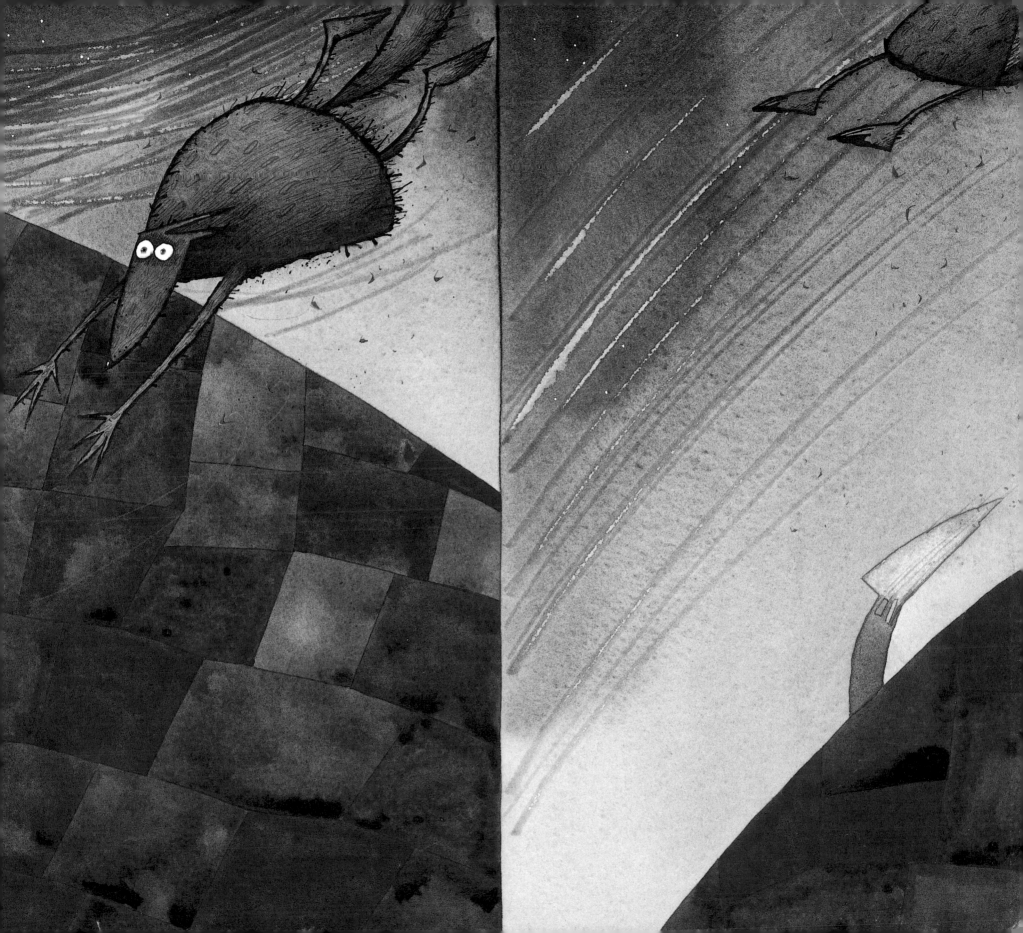

After all that fuss and fluster
Sam couldn't get to sleep,
until he closed his eyes and tried his best
to count his boring sheep...